Annie Trumbull Slosson

The heresy of Mehetabel Clark

Annie Trumbull Slosson

The heresy of Mehetabel Clark

ISBN/EAN: 9783743372771

Manufactured in Europe, USA, Canada, Australia, Japa

Cover: Foto ©Andreas Hilbeck / pixelio.de

Manufactured and distributed by brebook publishing software
(www.brebook.com)

Annie Trumbull Slosson

The heresy of Mehetabel Clark

THE
HERESY OF MEHETABEL CLARK

BY

ANNIE TRUMBULL SLOSSON
AUTHOR OF " SEVEN DREAMERS," ETC.

NEW YORK

HARPER AND BROTHERS

1892

THE HERESY OF MEHETABEL CLARK

WE had come to the mountains very early that year. It was only the first of June now, and we had been nearly three weeks among the northern hills. When we came old Lafayette wore a huge cap of dazzling white, and there was some snow upon the other mountains, and in hollows and shaded spots in the forests. But even then, in the earliest days of May, there were many signs of the coming spring—that spring of northern New England, whose slow, lingering, shy advance is so very beautiful.

The trees — except the evergreens — were leafless; but the hill-side forests wore that tender haze, or misty bloom, too faint and delicate to call color, but suggesting palest mauves and olives and grays, and here and there among them the swamp-maple showed its red buds.

Already the straw-yellow flowers of the adder's-tongue drooped above their odd, spotted leaves, and the wood anemone showed its frail white blossoms. The violets were out, too, the tiny, sweet white ones along the brook-sides, the round-leaved yellow ones in rocky places along the road, and selkirks with blue, long-spurred flowers peeping out where some little cold rill trickled slowly down from the mountain — a promise of the real spring; a mere whisper of a promise, but one sure to be fulfilled.

And now it was June, the very first of that lovely month, a warm, soft, sunny day, and we were spending it out-doors.

We were boarding in the village that season (in Franconia, I mean) at Deacon Whipple's—Deacon Seth, as he was always called, to distinguish him from Deacon Ephraim Whipple of the same town. He was not a native of Franconia, but was born in Sugar Hill, some three miles away, in the town of Lisbon, and to-day he was taking us out in his roomy, comfortable wagon to show us his native place.

Down the village street we went, past post-office and store and across the bridge over Gale River. Then we wound slowly uphill. The apple-trees were just coming into full bloom, the bird-cherries were losing their flowers, but the choke-cherries were white with spikes of feathery blossoms filling the air with their bittersweet scent. On we went, past meadows where the golden dandelions lay thick among the fresh young grass, pastures where the eyebrights clustered so closely that they looked at a distance like drifted snow; past brooks where the clear white water shone in the sunlight, and the blue and white violets peeped out along the banks. Maple, willow, elm, birch, beech and alder were all in full leaf now, and we drove along in a golden-green light, as the sunshine came down through the leaves. We were in no haste that day, and again and again we stopped to gather wild-flowers, ferns, or mosses, to chase a curious insect, or again to drop a line into a tempting hole under the shadow of a rock in Oakes's Brook. With tiarella, straw-lilies, gold-thread, trillium, cassandra, labrador tea, our hands and laps were soon full; and at our feet lay a big bunch of the rhodora, its leafless branches covered with lovely flowers of purple-pink.

Deacon Seth was a pleasant companion, and had a story for every spot on the way. He told us of the queer city-folks who sometimes came to the hotels which we were passing, and of the old days before those hotels existed. He pointed out the Salmon-hole Road, turning off at our right beyond Goodnow's, and related a thrilling incident of a drive down there on a night of storm and darkness. Then, as we came to the little school-house, he told a pathetic tale of a little daughter, Marietty, dead long years ago, but whose memory was as fresh and green in the old man's heart as the springing grass and budding leaves on this fair June day. Off there was the old gold-mine, which once raised such hopes and sunk so many dollars, and farther away, lying part in Lisbon and part in East Landaff, Ore Mountain, with its treasures of iron still hidden underground.

And so, through light and perfume and color and sound, sunshine and flower-scent, the green of leaf and bright tint of blossom, the song of birds and murmur of brooks, we came in sight of Sugar Hill Street. Such a tiny side-hill village it was, with its little church, post-office, store, and the few dwellings all on one road-like, downhill street. It was so quiet on that June day. As we drove along we saw no one, heard no sound of human life, except the laugh of one little rosy child, playing on the grass among the dandelions. A peaceful, restful little hamlet, it looked as if no sin or shame or strife could ever enter it, and one of us said so, as we looked from the green knoll on which the church stands, over the little village. Deacon Seth sighed heavily, was silent a moment, then turned and said, " Yes, it does look that way. I've often heard folks say that—boarders that I've fetched up here. I don't often say anything back, for I can't bear gen'rally to talk about it. But I don't seem to mind tellin' you, you're so much like our own folks, bein' here every year, and so on." He waited a minute or two, and we asked no question. Then he said, abruptly but solemnly, "For all it looks so peaceable and pious and soothin', yet right here, in this Christian community, under the shadow of this sanctuary, 's you might say, somethin' happened that went to show how Satan can find his way even into the godliest spot."

He lowered his voice, and, speaking almost in an awe-struck whisper, he said, "We had once, and for a long spell too, in our very midst and 'mongst, a heretic!" Pointing with his whip down the road, he added, "'Twas in that old red house. You see, it's a shop now — Ed Wilbur's joiner's shop; but it's standin' there still, a pillar and moniment, remindin' us allers, allers of that dreadful disgrace and sorrow."

And then he told us the story, told it as we drove slowly along, hour after hour of that summer day, over into the Landaff valley, on and on towards Bungay, and homeward to Franconia in the early evening. I shall try to tell it to you in his own words, with no comments of my own.

Deacon Seth had been brought up in that old New England school which so many of us remember, and which we recall with a certain tenderness after all, whatever now may be our varying creeds. It was a school of rigid, iron-bound formulas, which set forth what they who used them thought they ought to believe, rather than what they, in their good old hearts, really did believe. To them religion was not only dogmatic, but consisted wholly of dogmas; and belief in those dogmas was what they understood as saving faith. And he remained true to that ancient faith, which he was proud to call orthodoxy. Nor would he tone down or soften any of its asperities, make more gentle one of its stern expressions.

This was the deacon as a theologian. In daily life Deacon Seth Whipple was a genial, kindly, mellow soul, loving Nature in all her varied forms, and with a warm, soft heart for little children, and all weak, helpless things.

That he did not seem, while telling his story, to grasp the deeper meaning we found therein, and which I hope you, too, will see, was not owing to any lack of intellectual power. But he had been trained from his birth to see and walk in one narrow, strictly-bounded path, and he shut his eyes to any other as dangerous. I think, and you may also think, that he saw many of the truths that the story told us, otherwise his words could not have made us see them so plainly. But training, tradition, heredity, all forbade his acknowledging, even to himself, how much he saw.

"Her name— There, I knew you'd jump at that. Yes, 'twas a woman! I don't know why it seems so much worse for one of them to be an unbeliever, but it does, don't it, now? Both was made alike in the image of God, the Bible says; but somehow it's so everlastin' unnat'ral and queer for women folks not to believe things. Her name—as I begun to say afore—was Mehetabel Clark. She was daughter to Jephunneh Clark, one of the godliest men I ever see. Her mother, she come, too, of good, pious stock; she was a Quimby from Bethl'hem; and Mehetabel was raised in the most orthodox, straight up and down way. And she took to it from her birth, 'most. You couldn't hardly tell when savin' grace entered into her heart, for she was allers a pious, God-fearin' child, though she didn't become a perfessor till near twelve. When she was scurse thirteen I've heard her lead in prayer, and she knew her Bible by heart. And hymns!—why, she'd reel 'em off by the yard. She liked the best ones, too, the sound, good old-fashioned sort, that told what would happen to the unrepentin' sinner, and dwelt in poetry on the doctrines and decrees and judgments. They didn't have the wishy-washy stuff young folks sing to-day, and if they had had it, Mehetabel wouldn't have took to it, I know.

" She was well versed in the catechism, too—the Westminster Shorter. She knew all about foreordination and election and covenanted mercies before she could talk plain, and justification, adoption, and sanctification was as easy as A, B, C to Mehetabel allers. And she growed up into a girl, the same kind of solemn, sober-minded, religious young woman. Some folks thought she was too solemn for a young thing. She never went to parties or picnics or sleigh-rides, or any of them frolics among the young folks. She scursely ever laughed ; for you see she realized what a solemn thing life is, and that time is dread-

ful short at the best, and even three-score
and ten comes mighty quick, after all. And
as for me, I think it's a nice thing to see
youth feelin' that way. They don't much
nowadays; they're careless and light-
minded mostly, partic'lar the summer
boarders. She wa'n't a very happy person,
to be sure; but then we ain't meant to be
happy in this world; that wasn't what we
was made for. And it's a bad sign, I allers
say, to see any one feelin' too comfortable and satisfied. And though she seemed so religious and pious-minded to other
folks, she was forever mournin' over her
sins and fearin' she wasn't goin' to be
saved at the last. Sometimes she'd have
it that she'd committed the unpardona-
ble sin, and again, for a spell, that she
wasn't elected, and there wasn't any use
keepin' on tryin'. And then come up that
kind of nat'ral fear that she couldn't be
perfectly resigned and comfortable if she
knew she was condemned to eternal pun-

ishment, and she worried and fretted over that for a spell. That was foolish, of course, for I don't doubt she'd have took it all right and been as patient 's you please. I've seen a good many Christians in my time, young and old, but I've said time and again, and say it now, that I never see one that seemed to know better just exactly what a Christian had and hadn't ought to be than Mehetabel·Clark in them days. She had such a realizin' sense of God's justice and power and vengeance, why, 'twas a lesson to see and hear her. 'Twas beautiful, I tell you, such understandin' of His natur' and attributes in one so young. Of course she had her enemies, and things was said agin her; that was nat'ral. ' Blessed are them that are persecuted,' you know. In fact, I don't think she was a gen'ral fav'rite in Sugar Hill. The nat'ral heart, you see, and original sin accounted for that. She was a standin' reproof to all sinners, and

there was a good many there, like there
is in most places, and folks don't set much
by standin' reproofs. And the children
didn't like her, neither, and that was nat'-
ral, too. Children, unregen'rate ones, never do like the things they'd ought to like.
And to hear her talk to 'em of their prob-
'ble futur', and the dreadful outcome of
their doin's and not doin's, why, it kind
of made 'em uncomfortable. And I don't
think she liked 'em much, neither. It
pestered and worried her to see 'em goin'
on in their sinful ways, and her not able to
convince or convert. But if sinners didn't
think much of her, Christians did. All
the best and piousest of the church members set store by her, and admired to see
her grace and goodness. Elder Welcome
was settled here then, and he was a holy,
blessed man, if there ever was one. Dear,
dear, dear! when I see the ministers nowadays, and then think of him! Talk of
the Pope o' Rome, and how he has it all

his own way in his d'nomination, why, I
don't believe he's one-half so set as Elder
Welcome was, and I'm certain sure folks
don't give in to him so much. He ruled
Sugar Hill with a high hand, and a good
thing 'twas for us. And oh, such preachin'! None of the frivolous sort of discourses they call sermons in these days,
with stories and describin's and conver-
sations and all that throwed in to make
'em what they call interestin'. Interestin'! We don't go to meetin' to be interested; that's what I hold. If we want to
be interested, we can go to town meetin'
or vendues or closin' exercises at the
school. He give us every week, at least,
two good long discourses on the doctrines and beliefs of our d'nomination,
and he had 'em all himself at his tongue's
end, 's they say. Free-will and foreordination and effectual callin', perseverance
of the saints, the futur' state of unbap-
tized infants, and, above all, the natur'

and duration of eternal punishment, he'd give 'em to us week after week, often an hour and forty minutes at a talk, and they'd run off his tongue like ile. ▪ I never knew a man so grounded in all them things as he was. 'Twas the thing that allers struck folks most, after settin' under his preachin' a spell, how grounded he was in all the doctrines. When he died—a good many years ago 'tis now—if I'd a had my way, that's what they'd a put on his moniment, just that one word, 'Grounded.'

"Well, the elder he thought a heap of Mehetabel, and held her up as an example and model to the youth of the village, and he'd call on her frequent at evenin' meetin' to relate her experience and say a word in season to the light-minded and unconverted. I can see her now, standin' up in her pew, so straight and unbendin', with her white, mournful kind of face, and her black, scary lookin' eyes full of

wholesome fear of the Lord, talkin' of
her unworthiness, her vileness, the awful
things she deserved, and the willin'ness
she hoped she felt to bear 'em for endless
ages.   And she talked in such a wailin,'
doleful sort of voice, it made you feel
good an' creepy, like hearin' 'em sing
Windham or Chiny.   And speakin' of
singin' makes me think that Mehetabel
used to sing sometimes when she was all
by herself. She had a good ear, and could
catch a tune quick; and if she hadn't
known 'twas a sinful waste of time, she
could a gone ahead of most of the young
folks in music and all that.   But she
didn't see any harm in hymn-singin' when
she was by herself; and I've heard her,
time and time again, singin' low and soft
to herself those good and solemn psalms
and hymns they don't use enough nowadays. She knew all the different parts—
the treble and counter and all of what
they called, them days, fugein' tunes. But

2

she wouldn't sing 'em with other folks, for fear, as she used to say, 'twould be turned into a pleasure. So she took all the parts herself. One of her fav'rites was, 'Thy wrath lies heavy on my soul;' and when she'd come to the third line— you remember it, o' course—'While dust and silence spread the gloom,' she'd sing the tenor part first, 'While dust and silence,' way up high; then the treble, 'dust and silence;' then the counter lower down, 'dust and silence;' and then all together 's well 's she could do it, 'sprea-ea-ea-ed the glo-o-o-m.' And when she ended up on the last line, 'Descend around me to the tomb,' her voice would kind o' die out like the wind in the chimney stormy nights. Another one was, 'Lord, what a thoughtless wretch was I!' to old Greenwich, you know. 'Twas powerful wakenin' to hear her sing that about

 "'On slipp'ry rocks I see them stand,
 And fiery billows roll below.'

" And another was,

"'As on some lonely buildin's top
The sparrer tells her moan,'

to the air of 'Mournin swain'—you rec'-
lect.

"I've stood outside her window just
after dark—that was the time she gen'-
rally sung—and listened by the hour to
hear her sing the Judgment Anthem.
She'd go right through the whole thing
—it's a dreadful fugein' one, you know—
takin' one part after another, even the
bass, and goin' up and down and over and
'cross and back and for'ard till it most
took your breath away. You rec'lect that
part about

"'Lively bright horror and amazin' anguish
Stare through their eyelids while the livin' worm lies
Gnawin' within them.'

"It's a splendid piece, and she'd do it
so 's you could most see the whole thing.
And then often—it's kind of mean in me

to tell of it now, as 'twas to listen to it
then; 'twan't meant for me to see and
hear—she'd stop, and I could see her by
her candle cover her face up with her
hands, and groan out in a sort of solemn
fear; and I'd sneak off through the wet
grass with a kind of scary, pricky, goose-
fleshy feelin' all over me, partic'lar under
my hair.

" Well, here I am takin' up all this time
about the Mehetabel Clark of those days,
and 'most forgettin' the awful change that
come afterwards. But this I've been tellin' you helps to make the rest more strik-
in' and solemn; that is, if I've been able
to make you see her 's she was then, a pious, serious-minded young woman, with
every sign and showin' of bein' truly con-
verted, and of havin' cast away the works
o' darkness and put off the old man and
his deeds; one that was weighed down,
as I never see any one else weighed down,
with a proper and realizin' sense of her

own unworthiness, her guilty natur', and
the justice and jealousy and vengeance of
the great and awful God.   I say it again,
's I said it afore, 'twas beautiful, beautiful.
There was them — mostly rather luke-
minded sort o' Christians—that said there
wasn't love and charity enough in her for
the best kind of perfessor, and that she'd
a been more comfortable and not suffered
so much if she'd a had more.   That's all
foolishness, for the Bible says, you know,
that even charity itself 'suffereth long,'
and if she'd been chock-full of love and
charity she'd a suffered just as much from
knowing her own sin and wickedness.
Old Mis' Wells—she was one of your softly, pleasant, at-ease-in-Zion kind of folks
that never worried about her own soul
nor anybody's else's—she says to Mehetabel one time, says she, 'Couldn't you
jest try and love Him a little more, 's
well as fear him?'   And Mehetabel she
looked at her with her big black eyes,

and she says in her mournful voice, 'I ain't worthy yet to lift up my eyes to Him, much more to darest to love Him, me, the vilest thing He's made. I have give myself to Him body and soul, and he has accepted the worthless sacrifice. He has taken me out o' the horrible pit and out o' the miry clay, and there is none,' she says, loud and sharp, 'that can pluck me out of His hand. But He himself,' says she, 'can cast me into outer darkness, He can break me to pieces like a potter's vessel.'

"And so 'twas about the Scripters. She read them from mornin' till night, but 'twas most allers the Old Testament: the prophets, and so on. And when some carpin' and fault-findin' church member dealt with her about that, and argued that there was another part of the Bible that was pretty important and val'able to Christians o' the real sort, Mehetabel says, ' 'Tain't that I don't want to dwell on that part, nor that I ain't a longin' for the time when I can begin to look at that side o' the subjeck. But now, now, 'tain't for me. 'Twould make me too comfortable, and I'd forget my own sinful, wretched state. I'm glad there's them,' she says, 'that can read it and feel free to rejoice in its good tidin's, but 'tain't for me yet, 'tain't for me.'

"There, I guess you understand that part now, and you won't wonder at our all thinkin' that Mehetabel Clark was one o' them — as the catechism says — 'from all eternity elected to everlastin' life;' and believin' as we, most of us, did in the perserverance o' saints you'll see how unprepared we was for what come after.

"Well, Mehetabel was took sick, dreadful sick. That was after her father 'n mother 'd been dead some time, and she was livin' with Nathan, her married brother. I don't know what the matter was with her exactly—a fever, I guess, at the start; but she got worse and worse till every one see she was dangerous. They had old Dr. Thayer attendin' her reg'lar, but after a spell they called in Dr. Morse from Littleton, and then they had in some one from Haverhill, but none of 'em did a mite of good. She had her mind all through, and she was in the most proper and Christian state, prayin' out loud for mercy, bemournin' and bewailin' her sins, and tellin' all around her what a fearful thing 'twas to fall into the hands of the livin' God.

"But one night when I stopped, as I was drivin' home the cows, to ask about Mehetabel, they told me she'd sank into a kind of stupid, and the doctors thought she wouldn't ever come out of it. They scursely thought she'd hold out till mornin', but she did, and when I come home from the field, next afternoon, my folks told me she was still livin'. And she laid there day after day for nigh on a week, just that way as if she was dead, only she breathed. Nobody thought she'd ever rouse up, and it most seemed a pity she should. For while she laid there, so terrible still and dead-lookin', somehow she had a peacefuller, more comfortable look on her face than she'd ever had afore since she was a baby. I see her myself two or three times. Nothin' never disturbed her, so they let folks in 's much as they pleased, and everybody wanted to see her once more.

"She didn't look like Mehetabel some ways. That scary, solemn, anxious face went away, and, after a spell, she had a sort o' restin', satisfied, peaceable look on her featür's that we wasn't used to. And one after 'nother of us would turn away, our eyes pretty wet and our throats choky, and whisper 's we tiptoed out of the bedroom, 'Well, she's most there, and she looks it, every bit.' Dear me, dear me! If she'd only died then we'd a been 's certain sure of her destination 's of Paul's himself. But she didn't die. The doctors was wrong that time, and when her shroud was bein' made, and all the preparations for her funeral goin' on, one day, just about sunset, somebody happened to look at her, and they see her eyes was open, and there was sense in 'em.

"They sent in a jiffy for Dr. Thayer, and he come and looked her over, felt her pulse, and all that, and said she seemed to be stronger, she hadn't any fever, and he guessed there was some chance for her. They begun to feed her up and nourish her, and she gained and gained till there wa'n't any doubt of it—she was goin' to be spared to us. Well, we couldn't help bein' dreadful glad, even though 'twas keepin' her out of heaven a spell longer, as it seemed to us then. And you see we didn't at first, nor for quite a spell, find out about the awful thing that had happened to her, and the dreadful change that had come over her soul; for at first she didn't talk any. She seemed sensible and appeared to know folks, took her victuals and her physic when they brought 'em to her, but she never said a word; and all the time she kep' on wearin' that peaceable, satisfied, restin' look in her featur's that she'd had when she laid there so long—the look that was so different somehow from the Mehetabel Clark o' the old times. Now I can see, knowin' what come after, that that very thing ought to made us suspect something was wrong, but—well, it didn't, anyway. We'd ought to have knowed 'twas a bad sign for one that had allers had the fear of the Lord before 'em, and a realizin' sense of the awful value of life, to lose it all to once, and put on that comfortable, easy sort o' look; it seemed like false s'curity, like Mr. Vain Confidence in *Pilgrim's Progress*, you know. But we didn't any of us think o' that at first, we was

so glad to see her out of pain and sufferin'.

"I disremember now just how long
'twas afore we found out. When she begun to talk a little 'twas only about her
victuals or drinks or openin' the window
or shuttin' the door or something, and
we all see her head was straight and her
senses all there. They kept her 's quiet
's they could for a long spell. But one
day—I wasn't there myself, but I've heard
tell of it so many times seems 's if I was
—one day her sister-in-law, thinkin' 'twas
time she was roused up to her Christian
duties again, says to her, 'Mehetabel,
have you offered thanks to God for your
wonderful raisin' up 's from the grave?'

"Mehetabel looked up at her, just as
calm as ever, only a little mite puzzled
like, and she says, 'How, Jane?'

"Mis' Clark said it over, plain and loud-
er, thinkin' the sickness might a made her
a little hard of hearin'. And Mehetabel

she looked her right in the face, calm and sensible 's ever, and she says, 'I don't seem to know what you mean, Jane; who'd you say?'

" Well, well, Mis' Clark often said after that you could have knocked her down with a feather, she was so took aback and upset. But still she sort of hoped 'twas just because Mehetabel's mind wasn't quite clear yet, and that she'd come out all straight after a spell. But she didn't! That's what I've been comin' at with all this long story, and I suppose you see 'twas comin'. But it's just as hard for me to tell you, now I've reached the p'int, as if I hadn't led up to it. But 'twas so, and we all had to face it : her own folks, the minister, the church and society and her neighbors. She'd lost her religion, put her hand to the plough and turned back, become a backslider, a castaway; and, what's more, the dreadful and mysterious part of it was, she'd act'-

ally lost her belief in there bein' any God at all. She wouldn't hear of Him. She throwed away His holy word, she gave up prayer, abandoned the sanctuary, she —yes, there's no denyin' the terrible fact —she'd become what I begun by callin' her to you at the start, a heretic!

"She growed stronger, and at last got all well in body and mind, but her soul had got some dreadful hurt and it never healed over. Somehow in that sickness of hers she'd fell into the tempter's power, and yielded to him; she'd forbore to resist the devil and he hadn't fleed from her. Of course everything was done that could be. Elder Welcome labored with her for days and weeks and months; her own folks, the neighbors and friends and the church, all prayed and argufied, threatened and coaxed. They held special meetin's, had a day of prayer for her conversion; they sent for Mr. Martin, the great revivalist from Vermont, but it was labor throwed away. After all their talkin', and preachin', and prayin', she was still the same unbelievin' sinner, without hope, and without God in the world.

"No, mebbe it wa'n't that just exactly —that is, the first part of it. She was without God, poor, deluded creatur'; but as for hope, why, she'd got a queer, crazy kind of one that nobody understood or wanted to. There's no good in tryin' to tell about that; you couldn't make anything out of it, any more than we could, and it's neither here nor there. It's nothin' to do with the main p'int of the story; that is, the fact that she that had been a pillar of the church, a bright and shinin' light, a city that was set on a hill that couldn't be hid, she had become like the beast that perisheth, the fool that said in his heart there is no God. 'Twant anything but a kind of an idee, or a made-up story, I never could exac'ly make up my mind which. Sometimes I'd think 'twas the first, and that she really believed it, but then I see that couldn't be. She wasn't crazy; we all knew that. She was every bit as sensible, industrious a member of the c'mmunity as anybody there; did her house-work, her gard'nin', her knittin' and sewin' and mendin' as well 's she'd ever done 'em, and mebbe a mite better. She was as clear-headed and stiddy-goin' as she'd ever been, and every one of us see and knew it. So when she'd start off on this queer, ramblin' story of hers, without a fact in it as far as we could see, why, how could we help thinkin' that she'd made it all up delib'-rate, to sort of smooth over her awful unbelief, or divert folks's minds from it?

"This is all 'twas. She declared she'd been off somewheres—just where or when she never'd exactly tell; but it seemed to be quite a ways. From her talk it seemed to be out o' the United States, 'cross the water somewheres. But, dear me, how'd she expect us to credit a thing like that? She never in all her born days had been farther away than Concord, and that was when she was only six year old, so 't didn't make a lastin' impression. But nothin' she talked about in speakin' of that deestrict was anything like what went on in this country of ours. But 'twas a free country; we gathered that from what she let fall; for she didn't ever talk right out about it. I don't know 's she ever really said in so many words she'd been away to a foreign land, and seen this or that. But she talked about a strange, outlandish country, what she'd seen and what folks done there, and how she lotted on goin' back before long; and, above all—and that's how we come to think 'twas a free country—about the President and his son. My, my! how it does bring back Mehetabel just to say that! Why, I'm most ashamed to tell you that when I hear the President talked of I never think first of him that's our lawful ruler at Washington, or even of them that used to be there — Andrew Jackson or General Taylor and them. But I think o' Mehetabel Clark's President, one she made up out of her own head, and that didn't or couldn't, in the natur' of things, ever live anywhere in this mortal world. How she ever made up such a person, what she ever found anywheres to make him out of, beats me. It might have come out of some book o' travels or adventur's, shipwrecks and d's-asters, or castin' away on desert islands, or somethin'. But, then, she'd never read any books, nothin' much, but her Bible.

"But she had him complete, all out in her head, so that she knew just what he'd do or say or command or advise in any kind o' circumstances. And I must say 'twas a takin' sort of character, and made even us, that disapproved the whole thing, and never wanted to encourage

her talkin' about it when she'd ought to
have been thinkin' of her immortal soul
and what 'twas comin' to—why, 's I said,
it would make even us wish sometimes
that it was true, and that there was somewheres such a President and such a country. But, mercy me! to think of livin' on
a fairy-story like that, and givin' up your
religion for it and the fear of God. 'Twas
dreadful! But I haven't told you the very
worst part of it; that is, if it's right to say
worst when 'twas all bad and there wasn't
any best. But someways what appeared
to make it worse in one way, at least most
dangerous to other folks, was that in a
good many ways she was better than she
used to be; at any rate, more of a fav'rite.
And she was a heap happier, that's the
melancholy truth. O' course some of us
church members see how that could be—
that 'twas the false peace o' the wicked,
and she was self-deceived and sportin' on
the brink, as often happens. But to the

outsiders, seein' her allers calm and peaceful lookin' now, without that worried look
she used to have, and seein' her, too, so
good and pityin' to folks in trouble, and
so takin' with the children and youth, and
her a heretic, 'twas terrible dangerous.

"Why, in all her talks with the young
folks in them days I don't believe she
ever used the name of the God she used
to fear and worship, nor quoted the pas-
sages of Scriptur' she used to have at her
tongue's end. But it's only fair to say
that her conversation, puttin' aside that
awful leave-out, was good and improvin',
and the advice and suggestions and teachin's she give 'em, took,' s she said, from
the President or his son, couldn't be bet-
tered. 'The President says'— I can hear
her sayin' that now, in a kind of softly
way she had whenever she referred to
him, for she appeared to have the great-
est respect for him and what he said ; and,
wherever she got it, 'twas allers the wisest,

sensiblest, kindest talk she put into his mouth, I must say. And so folks got to goin' to her with their worries and troubles and sorrers and puzzlin's, and she allers had somethin' for 'em all that the President said, and that seemed to be just the thing for each partic'lar case.

"Where in the universe did she get some of those sayin's? She never'd been so dreadful smart, or took to eddication anyway, and as for books, as I've said before, she'd never read any but the Scriptur's, and mebbe, for a change, once in a good while, the *Pilgrim's Progress*. So her makin' up of all these things, which come in so pat and appropri'te every time, did seem mortal sing'lar, and some folks held that she couldn't a done it alone, and must have had somebody to help her. But brother Wilcox—he was the elder's great stand-by — said if she needed help, and he didn't think she did, for, says he, it's man's heart, and wom-

an's too, for that matter, that Scriptur'
says deviseth mischief continually, seeks
out many inventions and devises wicked
imaginations; but if she did need a help-
er she'd have found one, ready and willin'
enough; that old serpent which is the devil and Satan; Scriptur' again. And as for
it's all bein' good and moral what she
, made up, he went on, why, that difficulty's
got over by knowin' that the tempter can
take on the featur's of an angel,·and that
he sometimes, as we've warrant for sayin',
will even quote Scriptur' itself. Brother
Wilcox was allers hard on Mehetabel.

"I ain't givin' you yet much notion of
what her idees was, am I? But you see
it's so hard to tell just what she meant
I only know that she somehow or other
give us the idee that this President was
perfectly just every way; that he had strict
laws, but never made any that couldn't
be kep' somehow; that he had onlimited
pardonin' power, and, bein' very forgivin'

in his natur', he was allers exercisin' it.
But though she owned up that there was
ha'sh laws there, and folks had got to keep
'em or take the consequences, she never
seemed to like to dwell on that part.
She'd talk and talk by the hour about the
President bein' so good to the people, settin' by 'em and helpin' 'em and forgivin'
'em. Why, from her talk you'd think there
was more forgivin' and overlookin' and
passin' over things than anything else;
and while she was goin' over and over
that part you'd forget the laws and the
punishin's and the strictness and all that,
and just look at her fav'rite side of the
President—an awful lax one. But she
made it out all right, and you couldn't
help thinkin' while she talked that you
understood it all and that it could be
somehow. I said she didn't talk out the
whole thing in plain words, but let you
know it somehow from kind of hints and
allusions and so on. That was with grown

folks, and they never liked to ask her
questions right out. But 'twas different
with children. I forgot to tell you how
'twas that people let their children be
with such a dangerous character at all.
Well, at first they didn't, or they tried
not to. But the young ones was crazy to
be with her, and they'd slip off and go,
and bimeby their mas found that instead
o' doin' 'em any harm, she seemed to
make 'em better, as fur as this world was
concerned: more obedient and biddable,
and peaceable among themselves. And
the boys and gals did like so to go with
her, and they'd be took care of and out
o' mischief a whole afternoon if they was
with her; so folks give in and let 'em
go.

"And they'd ask questions — children
will, you know. My Marietty, she was
there a good deal, and she used to tell me
and ma about it, and for the life of us we
couldn't help likin' to hear; 'twas just a

most interestin' fairy story. 'Did you
ever see the President yourself?' they'd
say, after she'd been a talkin' about him
a spell; and she'd answer, sort o' hesitatin'
and slow, but in that same softly way she
always spoke about him, 'I think I did,
once,' she says; 'but whether I was in my
body or out o' my body I ain't certain
sure, but — the President knows.' She
says, 'I 'peared to be ketched up and took
way up, up high to the very top floor. I
think his son let me in, and then—I—
well, seems 's if I see him. But 'twas
more'n fourteen year ago,' she says, 's if
she was thinkin' and tryin' to rec'lect, 'and
I disremember just how it was. Mebbe
I was in my own body, mebbe I was out
o' my own body, I ain't certain sure, but—
the President knows.'

"'The top floor o' what?' some little
fellar 'd say, wantin' to know the whole
thing, as children will.

"'Why, the White House,' says she.

" 'Do they have a White House there, too?' the children says.

" 'Course they do,' says Mehetabel; 'and, oh, it's so white—whiter than the shiniest snow,' she says.

" 'And what did the President look like?' one of 'em inquires again, and she answers, 'Seems 's if I didn't see his face plain. If I rec'lect right, 'twas again' the law; but 't any rate nobody could look him straight in the face and stand it, made 'em so ashamed. But he passed by in all his strength and greatness and goodness and pleasantness, and I just hid away behind somethin', and didn't peek out till he'd got way by. But I see him in the distance, goin' from me,' she says, solemn and yet smily, 'and I sha'n't never, never forget it. And when I come away after that visit, why, they said my featur's was all shiny, and they was 'most afraid of me; but I never mistrusted that myself, till they told me a spell arterwards.'

" 'And didn't the President say noth-in' to you ?' they says.

" ' Oh yes,' she answers, 'most in a whis-per, 'but I couldn't put that into talk, and if I could you wouldn't understand. But, oh yes, he spoke to me that time, and lots of times arterwards, and his voice sounded like the noise the wild Amonoo-suc and Gale River and Salmon Hole Brook and Swift Water makes, all goin' at once ; loud, you know, and rushin' and ringin' and clear. And again 'twas like a big wind in the pine-trees over there in the grove, and sometimes it sounded like a trumpet blowin'. Another time when he was speakin' folks would think it thundered, the voice would sound so strong and powerful, and shake 'em so. But, then, more times, as it seems to me when I think it over, 'twas just a low, small, little voice that even the children could listen to and like to hear.'

" ' Wasn't the children afraid of him,

Aunt P'niel?' they'd say. There! that
makes me think that I've left out somethin'. Why, she was that unwillin' to remember the days when she was a trem-
blin', fearful believer that she'd even gone
and changed her name. Her story was
that the President done it; said 'twas the
custom there to give 'em new names, and
hers, for all the world, was Peniel. Cu-
r'us name that was; it's in the Bible.
But she allers called herself that, and
some folks humored her by usin' it. I
never did, and Elder Welcome didn't.
No more did the best church members.
But the children took it up, as young
ones will take up anything new, and so
she was 'Aunt P'niel' to them forever
after. And so, 'Wasn't the children
afraid of him, Aunt P'niel?' says they.

" 'Afraid o' the President!' says she,
'most laughin', 'the idee! Is Joey Barnes
afraid of his pa, or Mary Jane Frink scaret
of her mother?' They was both only

children, you see, and their folks set dreadful store by 'em. ' Why,' she says, ' it growed to be a sayin' all through that country, in speakin' o' the President, that he felt for his people just as a father would feel to pity his boys and gals. And there was another proverb, somethin' about his comfortin' folks as your mothers does you young ones when you're out o' sorts and fretty. And they had all sorts o' names for him, his people had, that showed pretty plain how they felt about him. I know one told about his bein' like a man that kep' sheep and lambs, that pastur'd 'em in the grassiest medders, and took 'em out along the brook to drink, and if the littlest lambs got tired he'd jest carry 'em and cosset 'em. And somebody else said he allers made him think of a great big bowlder that 'twas so nice to see on a hot, burnin' day, for it throwed such a big shadder, and cooled off and rested ye, when ye set down under it. Says another, "Yes, he is like a shadder, as far as coolin' and shadin' and restin' ye goes, but he allers strikes me," he says, "as bein', on the whole, more like the sun, so cheerin' and bright and shinin', and keepin' away the dark and scariness and worry from his people." And some held he was like a river, refreshin' the land, ye know; and some that he made 'em think of a spring o' nice, cold, clear water when ye was thirsty, and — oh, there ain't any name too good for them folks to call the President by, they was that fond of him, and set by him so.'

"'And what did you think he was like, Aunt P'niel?' they'd ask her.

"'Well, deary,' she'd say, 'he 'peared to me like all of them things at one time or 'nother, 'cordin' as you felt to want this or that in him. But somehow I most gen'rally held to the the'ry o' his fav'rin' the sun. For ye see we'd had a dreffle dark spell o' weather here afore I went there, and there wa'n't much difference 'twixt day and night for the longest time, and I'd got so sick and tired of it all, never seein' anything plain, and gettin' scaret at things I thought I see and heerd, that when I come there to the President's country—it's a terrible open, light, sightly place—why, I thought more of its bein' so sunshiny and clear, and having plenty o' light to see by, than I done o' anything else. So I liked to think of him as bein' like the sun, settin' the most store 's I done by that.'

"And so she'd go on and on by the hour, and the children drinkin' it all in like law and gospel. And 'twas, as I said afore, mortal takin'. I didn't know I could rec'lect so much of it, but it all comes back, as I tell it, like a real thing I seen somewhere myself, instead of just a made-up yarn told by a unbeliever.

"Now I know what you're thinkin'.

Several people have said it, and I ain't such a fool as not to see it myself, that there's some kind of a likeness 'twixt things she said and parts o' Scriptur'. That about the keepin' sheep, and so on, is something like the Psalms, you see. Well, of course it was nat'ral for one brought up as she was, from her youth, like Timothy was by his grandmother Lois and his mother Eunice, to search the Scriptur's; of course, I say, she couldn't help fallin' by spells into Bible language. But 'twas a mixed kind of Scriptur', and she twisted and turned it out of all likeness to the real thing to fit into her story. She knew what Scriptur' was as well as I do. And as for callin' a thing Scriptur' religion that hadn't a speck of anything doctrinal such as she was raised on, and that Elder Welcome had preached to her from her birth 'most, why, you see yourselves, it ain't likely. No, she was like them Paul speaks of, that havin' swerved, turned aside into vain janglin'; and vain janglin' 'twas, sure enough.

"I've left one thing out; I don't exac'-ly know how to tell that part. But in one way 'twas the most partic'lar part of her story; everything seemed to hang on it, and yet she never explained it right out. 'Twas only this, as she put it: the President had a son. There, that shows what example and habit can do! You see how I dropped my voice and spoke solemn when I said that. Well, Mehetabel allers used to do so. She never said a word about that part that her voice didn't get low and whisp'ry, as if some one was asleep or—had died. I never did understand how, someways, without sayin' anything really def'nite and plain, she could make everybody, me and all, feel that there was somethin' so dreadful solemn, drawin', and takin', and above and over all terrible important in that fact about the President's havin' a son. 'Twas the

4

only thing she ever seemed to cry about
—she took life so easy after her sickness
—that part about the President's son.
Her eyes would water and her mouth get
trembly, and it seemed 's if she couldn't
hardly speak about it. Sometimes, when
she'd say something comfortin' or helpin'
to somebody that come to her, as folks
got in the way of doin' when things went
wrong, they'd ask her, 'Are them the
President's words, Aunt P'niel?' And
she'd say, ' Yes, they be—or leastways his
son's. And you know,' she allers put on,
'that's just the same. What the President's son says, why, that's what the President means. He allers told us, the President did, to take anything his son said 's
if he said it himself; he was responsible
for it, every word, don't ye see?' Folks
said it allers seemed to them as if she got
the two mixed up somehow, and didn't
scursely know 'em apart herself.

" Yes, I heard what you said just now.

You quoted that verse about seein'
through a glass darkly, and I know what
you mean. You think she'd got the right
idee, after all, only a little mite skewed
and out o' shape by the twist-up in her
head after her sickness. Folks has said
it afore. But don't you see that's a dan-
g'rous thing to hold? Accordin' to that,
anybody might make up a story o' their
own, if 'twas only founded on fact and
with a sort o' Scriptur' flav'rin' to it; and
though every single savin' doctrine was
left out, you'd say 'twas religion, only
looked at through dingy, dull kind o'
glass. Elder Welcome talked about that
a good deal to such folks, and made 'em
see what things might come to if they
was too tol'rent and easy-goin' with
schism and wrong views and all. So they
put the thing down with a high hand,
called it infidelity right out in so many
words, just for the good o' the church
and community.

"But God makes use of sing'lar tools sometimes, and turns the weakest, mistakenest things into means o' grace and glory. And so He done in this case. I can't begin to tell you how many times He brought good out o' evil, and made the words and doin's o' this poor benighted woman bring forth fruit for His own vineyard. As the Bible rightly says, 'The wrath o' man shall praise Him.'

"'Twas dreadful queer; nobody seemed to take in her story as real true, or subst'ute it, as she appeared to do, for orthodox religion and a belief in the Almighty. Not a soul of 'em—except, perhaps, some of the children, such as is allers ready to swallow fairies and giants and ghosts—not a single soul really believed in her President and his son, and all she told of them and their country. But someways, after hearing her talk, I don't know how it was, folks used to find somethin' different and somehow more fillin' and satisfyin' in their own religion, as if they'd learnt somethin' new out of this crazy story. I suppose God done it, and made 'em see and hear somethin' different from what she really said, just as in the Scriptur's somewhere He made folks think they heard an army comin' when there wasn't any sign o' one. And so they really sometimes got good out of it. And there was one thing: she never said one word against anybody else's religious beliefs, whatever they was, only she never appeared to take much notice of 'em, or even rec'lect she'd ever held any of 'em herself.

"My Marietty—the little gal I lost, ye know—she got into a very low-spirited state once. There was a revival here, and she was impressed and under powerful conviction o' sin for a long spell. She was about twelve year old and wasn't very rugged, and she took everything pretty hard, and she went about for days,

lookin' so white and scaret and sorrer-
ful; she couldn't get peace anyhow. And
it seemed to make Mehetabel feel dreadful. I don't know why she should a took
it to heart so, but she told Marietty it
made her think of a gal she knew once
that looked just that way and felt just as
bad.

"'And did she ever get any peace?'
says my poor little gal.

"'Oh yes,' said Mehetabel.

"'Oh, please, how was it?' asks Marietty.

"'Why, 'twas just comin' to know the
President and his son,' says Mehetabel,
'and gettin' fond of them.'

"'Oh dear!' the child cries out, 'I wish
there was really a President! But there
ain't, there ain't, Aunt P'niel, there's only
just the great and awful God, and I can't
get fond of Him; I'm only scaret of Him.'

"Mehetabel looked so dreadful sorry
and pitiful, and she put her hand on Ma-

rietty's arm and stroked it, and she says, her voice all shaky, 'You poor, dear little creatur', I can't show you how to get fond of any one you're so scaret of, but I could if he only had—a son !'

"Wa'n't that a sing'lar coincidence? It reminded that child o' somethin' she'd forgot, and God turned it to His own glory. And when me and ma was in our room that evenin', about sundown, prayin' God to show the child His awful power and break her heart o' stone, she come in, her face all smiles and peace, and we see He'd done it.

" She died less than two year after that, Marietty did, and we buried her in the little graveyard back there. I meant to show you the very spot, with the cinnamon roses all 'round it. And we was so glad, me and ma, when that time come, thinkin' that anyway she was all right, let alone what we down here was feelin', that we allers felt someways obligated to the one that seemed to have a hand in bringin' her into the blessed light. Though of course we held Mehetabel Clark was only the unknowin' tool God used to show His own power.

" It was a good thing for the poor creatur' that the young ones, and weak, easygoin' growed folks did take so to her; elseways she'd a been dreadful lonesome. For she was given up, after a spell, by all the orthodox people, even her own relations. Of course, as she didn't go to meetin', Sundays, or assisted at any o' the stated means o' grace, it couldn't be expected that the church and society could let things go on as if nothin' had happened. Elder Welcome and all of us had set so high by Jephunneh and Mis' Clark that there wasn't any public trial and putin' out. But they just dropped her name off the roll. A committee waited on her and broke it to her as mild as they could consistent. But they needn't have worried about hurtin' her feelin's overmuch, for she didn't appear to take any interest in the subjeck. Just think of that now! What an awful change from the days when, as the good old hymn says, ' How pleased and blest was she to hear the people cry!' and so on; the time when she could say she 'had been there and still would go; 'twas like a little heaven below!'

" There was one thing, however, that showed the power of habit and the good of trainin' up a child the way he should go. She did make a kind of difference still between the Sabbath and week-days. But dear me ! 'twas a heathen sort of difference, and nothin' to do with keepin' the day holy. She didn't do any housework much that day; she used to put on her best, or anyways her cleanest clothes, and—well, we never knew just what she did do. She was up in her room a good deal, and when the children asked her what she was doin' there, she only said she had a great deal to think about, things the President and his son had mentioned to her, and she was afraid she might forget 'em, and unmeanin' talk like that. And when the young ones asked her why she couldn't think just 's well down in the settin'-room, if they wouldn't make a noise or talk to her, she said no, she'd gathered from things the President said that 'twas safer to latch herself in. But 'twasn't for much good, I'm afraid, those times up there, not a bit like the old seasons of self-examination, penitential mournin', and solemn fear she used to spend. For whereas in those past times she'd come out with her featur's all drawed, showin' what terrible dealin's she'd had with the tempter, she'd come down-stairs now, lookin' so cheerful and pleased and comfortable-like, you never'd dream 'twas the Sabbath day from her face and general appearance. And she'd get the children together then, and tell 'em stories, not Bible ones, but made-up stories, and not even a moral lesson at the end to count'ract the pleasure the story-part give 'em. We never let Marietty go on the Sabbath day, though she wanted to, even after she become a perfessor; and the best brought-up children wa'n't any of 'em allowed. But the lax folks settled things somehow with their consciences, and shut their eyes to their young ones' runnin' off there. So of course it come about soon that those children lost their wholesome fear and dread of the Lord's solemn day, and looked for'ard to it as they might a done to singin'-school or goin' out to take tea, which was terrible demoralizin', you see. As far 's I know she didn't let 'em play games or things like that. The boys and gals would tell my Marietty about their times there, and when she was teasin' to go she'd repeat 'em to me and ma. She

said Marthy Welles was talkin' about it
one day, at recess, and she said 'twas
dreadful interestin' the stories Aunt
P'niel told 'em about the President and
his son and the White House and all.

"'Why, them ain't Sunday stories,'
says Ansel Peabody, Deacon Veranus
Peabody's little boy, 'and it's wicked to
have any but Bible stories that day; pa
says so.'

"'I know 'bout that,' says Marthy,
lookin' a little mite ashamed, 'but if you
won't tell—we don't want Aunt P'niel to
know—but we thought we'd make it so's
it wouldn't be wicked by just makin' believe she was tellin' us about Heaven;
and so we play she is, and it 'most seems
sometimes 's if that was the way 'twould
be up there, and I wish 'twas — there!'
She was a spunky little piece, and didn't
really mean it, of course. Moses Welcome took that up in a jiffy. He was
the minister's son, and the only child in

Sugar Hill that hadn't ever been let go
to Mehetabel's since her fall. And Moses says, when he heard Marthy Welles
say that about Heaven, 'Oh, Marthy,
Marthy!' pointin' his poor spindlin' finger
at her, his peaked little white face all
ha'sh-lookin' from godly wrath, 'how
could you play about such a solemn lo-
cal'ty as Heaven! Anyways, you must
see how diff'ent 't is from the place that
unbelievin' woman tells about, where the
children play in the streets and sing and
ask the President and his son for everythin' they want, not the leastest speck
scared of 'em. What you been a-listenin'
to Sabbath days when my pa described
that solemn place, not to know no better
than that? There ain't no playin' or
talkin' and askin' for things up there,' he
says. 'Folks jest set still in rows forev-
ernevernever, 'cause it's a never-endin'
Sabbath, you know. And as for that she
said about puttin' his arms round 'em

and them a-smilin' up to him, why, Marthy Welles, you'd oughter know they never smile in Heaven!'

" I tell you, 'twas as good as a whole sermon on the occ'pations and solemn employments of that glorious abode to hear that youthful Christian. 'Out o' the mouths o' babes,' you know.

" I told you that she was given up by her relations as well as by the Church. Course I don't mean that her brother and his wife turned her out-doors. But I guess they couldn't help lettin' her see what a trouble 'twas to have an unbeliever and scoffer in their own Christian household. So it come about before long that Mehetabel took that little house I showed you in the village that's a shop now, and there she lived, all by herself at first. But she never appeared to be lonesome much. The children were in and out all the livin' day, and folks in affliction or ailin', that wa'n't up to doin' their every-day work, would drop in and talk for want of anythin' better to do. Then she said, in her crazy way, that she heard frequent from the President and his son, though we never knew of her receivin' a letter from year's end to year's end.

"She went around a good deal. That was so queer, for before her sickness she used to be such a stay-in, except for goin' to the sanctuary. She didn't go there now, as I said, nor to sewin' society, or female prayer-meetin', or anything stated like that. But she got to be a real gadder 's fur as pryin' into queer places. If there was an accident, folks hurt or crippled, or even a horse or cow or dog or cat with anything the matter, Mehetabel was sure to be there. And as she seemed, after all, to be handy now in sickness and such, why, folks would let her stay round and help.

"The oddest places she'd go to. Why, when that man I was tellin' you about—

Dexter, you know, that robbed the store —was took up and lodged over night in the lock-up, or lobby, as we call it round here, what did Mehetabel Clark do but go and see him. And when somebody asked her about it, she made up some story or other about havin' been to see the President's son. And when some one taxed her right out with havin' been to peek in on and pester that poor thief Lot Dexter, she owned up, but got round it by sayin' that 'twas the same thing after all as if she'd been visitin' the President's son himself. And she'd make that same excuse about goin' to see sick folks, even perfect strangers, or talkin' to tramps, and takin' them into her house. No matter how barefaced it was, everybody seein' and knowin' it, she'd allers say, as calm and quiet 's could be, that she'd been doin' this or that, whatever it might be, to the President's son. Some folks that wasn't perfessors talked a good deal about the good she done this way, but Deacon Priest used to shake his head and say, 'Works, works.' He was a master-hand for poetry, and he'd put on

'The best o' deeds
Is nothin' but weeds
Alongside o' doctrines, confessions, and creeds.'

"Then she changed so about wastin' her precious time, and takin' to friv'lous pursuits. She begun to take such notice of what folks call scenery, the mountains and the streams and woodsy places, and even the clouds, sun-risin's, and so on. Why, of course God made all those things, and they 'd ought to fill us with a realizin' sense of His power. What is man? and all that, as the Bible says. But as for settin' for hours lookin' at the mountains, when you've seen 'em every day of your livin' life—and if there's a mortal thing that's just the same allers and never alters any with age or anythin', it's

5

mountains—why, it's well enough for summer boarders off on a vacation with nothin' else to do, but it's dreadful foolish and time-wastin' for workin' folks. But Mehetabel, she'd go off to some sightly spot, like that place where you stopped me, back there, before we got up to Sugar Hill Street, and there she'd stand or set, and look and look off at the mountains. She went alone a good deal, but sometimes she'd take the children.

"'What makes you like to look at the mountains so much, Aunt P'niel?' they says sometimes, and she'd smile and say, 'They make me think o' the President's land somehow.'

"'Was there mountains there?" they says.

"'Oh yes,' she answers; 'they was all round the city—outside, you know ; and the White House itself was on real risin' ground, such a viewly place. Why,' she says, smilin', 'it does seem so dreadful

queer for you to ask if there was mountains there, when the first thing you'd take
notice of, 'most, was its bein' such a hilly,
high-ground deestrict. Why, even here
in Sugar Hill it 'pears flat and low when
I rec'lect the President's land, and I
come out here and look at Lafayette and
Kinsman, and all these Francony hills,
and think and think of the President's
mountains and the land that seems sometimes so dreadful fur off.'

"'I don't like to look at the mountains,' says Ansel Peabody; 'they make me
think o' how we'll be callin' on 'em some
day to fall on us an' cover us, when
the judgment comes, you know; and
how they thundered and lightened and
smoked up and earthquaked in com-
mandment times, and—oh, I tell ye they
scare me, and I try not to think of 'em
after dark!'

"'Why, you poor young one!' says Mehetabel; 'they make me think o' such dif-

f'rent things: how they don't change no more'n the President does; how kind o' quiet and restin' and peaceful they be. And I rec'lect some o' the sayin's they had there, about how the President was all 'round his folks, takin' care on 'em allers, just as the hills was round the town; and another about how they fetched peace to all the people that lived among 'em. And I remember — oh, such pleasant, beautiful things that happened on hills and risin' ground! The President set lots o' store by 'em himself, and deary me! there wasn't never any one who was more fond o' mountains than the President's son. When I come up here all by myself, times, you know, when I tell you I don't want you for a spell, why them times I am rec'lectin' things about him.

"'And when I feel lonesome or tired or worry a mite about things, I jest raise my eyes up to them hills, and it helps me lots. And if I'm real comfortable and

happy—as I allers most gen'rally be, somehow—why, I look at 'em till it seems as if
they'd most bust right out into singin'
tuncs, or 's if they'd jump for joy like,
and the leastest ones, like Bald Mountain
and such, would dance about like cossets.'

"You see, every once in a while she'd
kind of slip into Scriptur' from force of
habit, I suppose. But as she didn't remember 'twas Bible language, and as she
put it into plain Sugar Hill talk in the
most sacrilegious way, why 'twas worse
than not usin' it at all. But the only
time I ever heard her quote a verse lit'-
ral, was about the mountains, too. But
that wasn't exactly appropri'te, and didn't
mean much.

"You see them two banks of snow up
there on Lafayette? Yes, the White Cross,
as you call it; I don't. It's nothin' in the
world but a long, deep holler up there,
where the water runs down in a wet spell
and makes a watercourse, and that holler

cuts right through a stony ledge up there, and runs slantin' down. The whole place is in the shade, and don't ever get the sunshine. So it stands to natur' that the snow lays in the holler and at the foot of that ledge pretty late in the spring, and don't melt till after it's gone from all round it. And so that holler and the bottom of the ledge looks white again' the mountain, and as they run acrost each other, so—like the sticks of a kite or a cross, if you want to say so—why, folks call it the White Cross, as you did just now. I never call it that myself, for I believe in givin' things their right names, and not coverin' them all over with imaginin's and make-believes; but if there's any class of folks that always imagine a vain thing, as the Bible says, it's boarders. To me that thing up there is just snow in a holler and under a ledge of rock. I've been up there myself and know what it is really; and I don't want to play it's anything different. If I did, why I'd be more likely to feel like little Ansel Peabody, and think of the rocks rendin', and the wrath of the Lord breakin' the hills asunder. The first time Mehetabel saw it—that is, after she was sick and lost her religion—it seemed to make a great impression on her. Some of the children was with her that day. 'Twas the last of May, and there'd been a fortnight of rainy, foggy weather, so that the tops of the mountains had been covered with clouds for days and days.

" It cleared off that mornin' while Mehetabel was standin' out there on the hill with the children, and the fog and mist went off the top of Lafayette, and the sun shone on that holler and the ledge of rock where the snow was layin'. And as she saw it it seemed to remind her of somethin' in that crazy dream of hers. And she called out, with the tears runnin' down her cheeks, ' He lifteth up an ensign on the mountains.' That's in Isaiah, and she'd read it in old times. And when the young ones asked her what she meant, and what she was cryin' for, she kep'sayin', over and over, 'It's their flag! It's the flag o' the President and his son!'

"She seemed more excited and stirred up than they'd ever seen her, Marietty said, for she was most gen'rally quiet and even-like since her sickness. She drawed the boys and gals close up to her, and pointed to that holler and ledge with the snow shiny-white, and told 'em how somethin' like that was the sign or mark—colors, I suppose she meant—of the land where she'd been; how it was on everythin' there, on the banner over the White House that they set up in the name of the President and his son, and how the soldiers carried it, and all the people wore it. And Marietty said that while she was talkin' about it her hands shook and her eyes was wet, and yet her face looked all lit up in the sunshine, as she went on about how all the folks loved that sign, and wore it and fought for it and, so she said, died for it sometimes.

"'Do you wear it, Aunt P'niel?' says one of 'em.

"Her face looked a mite troubled for a minute. 'I want to,' she says. "It's my sign; I b'long under it, and I'd die for it in a minute, if it come to that. But,' she says, hesitatin' a little bit, 'I've allers heerd that 'twas kind o' heavy, and it hurt to wear it, even if the President and his son fitted it on to you theirselves. And nothin' hurts me nowadays, and I hain't got anything hefty to carry, I'm sure. So mebbe I ain't got the right kind yet. You ain't never,' she says, lookin' kind o' sharp and close into their faces— 'you ain't seen me, dearies, look 's if I was carryin' somethin' sharp and hefty, have you?'

"'Why no,' says they, and Almy Smith,

who was allers speakin' before she stopped to think, puts in, 'No, ma says you look a terrible sight comfortabler and pleasanter than you did before you backslid, and she thinks it's queer, too, when your folks has give you up and turned you out, and the meetin' folks won't have you belong to 'em, and all that.'

" 'Oh, that ain't anythin',' says Mehetabel, 'jest givin' up your folks. I'd do more'n that for the President and his son, jest to give up my folks. But I hope I'll get the real sort o' sign to carry about some day! One that's hefty, you know, and hurts.'

" When Moses Welcome heard all about that—the snow on Lafayette and what Mehetabel said about it—he went to his pa with it. And the elder told him not to be repeatin' things like that, for 'twas popish talk and very dang'rous.

" Well, after that she set everything by that white mark on the mountain. It only lasted a few days that year, before the thaw took it away, but she was out lookin' at it every minute she could get.

"She had to work pretty hard after she left her brother's. She had a little garden and raised her own roots : potaters and turnips and such ; and she took the whole care of that. Then she pulled rugs and sewed rag carpets, and did little things like them, so as to keep along somehow, and it didn't take much to keep her. But 'twas dreadful queer how she could give away so much out of her livin' to the poor and the children and so on. And bimeby, of all things in the world, she took in a poor creatur' to do for and keep. There was some Injuns from Canada come down here one summer with baskets to sell to the boarders, and one of 'em, an old woman they called Tury, she was took terrible sick. And the other Injuns, in their hard-hearted kind of way, they just went off, and left her without a cent or any one to take care of her. Mehetabel, she heard about it, and she went right down to the place where she was; they'd had a camp and a tent, and they'd left old Tury right there on some straw or something; and while the men folks was discussin' what town she belonged to, and what to do with her, she fetched her home. She nursed her up and took care of her as if she'd been her mother or something or other to her, and when Tury got well, why they just stayed on together the rest of their days.

"You see Mehetabel really was good natur'd and never wanted to see any one sufferin', if she could help it. But that was natur', not grace, and didn't count for much.

"Then Tury didn't cost her a great deal, for she was a handy old creatur' and did all she could to help, and she knew how to make baskets and learnt Mehetabel how, and that helped along some.

But the real reason that Mehetabel kep'
her, as I always held, was, after all, to pros-
elyte's you might say. You see she hadn't
ever had one follerer in that silly idee of
hers, and every livin' soul that has an idee
of his own, or a set of idees, call 'em art'-
cles of faith, or creeds, or the'ries, or anything you please, he don't find much ex-
citin' or rousin' in it unless he has some
kind of follerin', some one he can learn
his beliefs to, and have for a disciple.
Now Mehetabel hadn't ever had a single
one really before. The children listened
to her and liked to, but they were all from
orthodox families, even the laxest of 'em,
and didn't really believe the yarns she
told.

" But Tury was a heathen, I suppose, if
she was anything. She was a poor, foolish, ignorant old thing. Whether she was
really what you might call 'lackin'' or
not, I can't exactly say, for she was the
only Injun I ever knew much, and mebbe

they're all that way. She talked a kind of outlandish lingo, but after a spell she picked up some talk you could understand, such as it was. So here was a terrible good chance for Mehetabel to get a follerer, for Tury hadn't any set beliefs, never'd been connected with any church or been grounded in any of the doctrines, and 'd just as lief take up with a false religion and antichrist ast he real thing. And she did take up with it dreadful easy. You see she got sort of fond of Mehetabel when she was takin' her in and doin' for her, time she was sick and deserted, and she was ready to believe anything she told her to believe. So by the time Elder Welcome was ready to begin a systematical course, as he called it, of religious teachin', why he found she'd swallered all that story about the President and the White House and the President's son, and he couldn't make any impression on her poor, hardened, deluded natur'. I heard him tell about his first past'ral visit, and the talk he had. Of course he begun with the law, her sinful state and just deserts, for conviction comes before conversion you know, and if ever there was a class of folks who are steeped in original sin and nat'ral depravity it's Injuns, I suppose.

"But Tury didn't appear to be weighed down any with a realizin' sense of what he said about her sins. She was a polite old creatur', and she listened and nodded her head and kep' still till he stopped to take breath. Then she says, in her odd Injun lingo, 'Yes, Tury bad, much bad, but Tury not know. Tury know now; sorry, much sorry. Misser Pres'dent und'stan'; son tell him 'bout Tury. He say all right, all right; poor Tury; Tury like me now. Tury like him lot. Tury be good now;' and on and on that foolish way, till the elder see 'twa'nt any use no more'n castin' pearls before swine; she was as set in her way of stickin' to that story of the President as Mehetabel Clark herself.

"I said that Mehetabel never had but one out-and-out follerer; no more she hadn't, in one sense. But there was one other person that took her story for true, or 't any rate acted 's if he did, or 's if he understood it all and didn't object to it. That was a summer boarder. He was a kind of minister that come every year to Sugar Hill for his vacation, not bein' very rugged in his throat, I believe. I never knew just what specie of minister he was, for I never see one exactly like him. He wasn't a Congo, as we call 'em round here, nor a Methodist, nor a Baptist, nor a Advent. He was more, in some ways, like a Cath'lic priest, but he wasn't that neither. Some said at first that he was a 'Piscopal, but he wasn't any more like old Mr. Miller, the 'Piscopal minister of Hold'ness, in clothes, or looks, or actin',

than he was like Elder Welcome. Come
to find out he had been a 'Piscopal, but
he'd been promoted, and he'd gone up so
high that they'd most lost sight of him.
He'd had his schoolin', folks said, acrost
the water, and that helped to make him
queer. He dressed kind of uncommon,
very stiff and straight and narrer and up
and down, some of his clothes fast'nin'
behind 'stead of front; he was pretty
pale and real poor lookin' in flesh, and he
had a good many odd ways and manners.
But I will say he was a nice, pleasant-
spoken, kind sort; and did a good deal for
Sugar Hill folks of all d'nominations.
Well, whatever his own religion and belief was, 'twas something that didn't pre-
vent his takin' in Mehetabel Clark's story,
or, any way, humorin' her and makin' her
think he believed it.

"He boarded at Mis' Deacon Peabody's
—she was one of the female pillars of the
church—and so it come about that she

6

told him about the disgrace on the c'mmunity, and the unbeliever in our very midst, thinkin' mebbe Mr. Latham—that was his name—might know how to deal with her. He was real interested, and he went to see her. Of course, nat'rally, I don't know just what took place between 'em at that time; but Mis' Deacon Peabody—she happened to be in Mehetabel's yard when he come out, though she hadn't heard any of the conversation—she said Mr. Latham's eyes looked wat'ry, as if he'd had rather a painful season. And when she asked him if he'd succeeded in openin' Mis' Clark's sin-blinded eyes any, he only said in a low voice somethin' she didn't quite catch, about some one else havin' done that for her a'ready, and hurried away.

"After that he was always goin' to see Mehetabel, or P'niel as he took to callin' her, seein' that pleased her. And folks said 'twas the craziest thing out of a

'sylum to see them two settin' there together by the hour, talkin' talk that nobody but themselves could understand,
with old Tury puttin' in a outlandish
word now and again, as if she follered it
all. I really do think Mehetabel made him
a little out of his head like. His brains
wasn't over strong anyway; he'd used 'em
a good deal—a thing brains wasn't meant
for, seems to me; and all this talk and
story and so on of this lost sheep went to
his head. Mis' Peabody says so to him
once in a kind of warnin' way, and he only
laughed in a sort of 'sterical way like a
nervy woman, and says, 'Went to my head!
To my heart, you mean, my good woman.'

"In spite of all this tamperin' with sin,
and humorin' a backslider just out of
what's called kindness and good-natur',
I don't doubt that Mr. Latham was a real
Christian. He seemed, 's far as we could
tell, to be orthodox and sound on the great
p'ints of doctrine, and he was a god-fearin',

serious-minded man. He didn't have a good mem'ry, nor much invention, any more 'n most 'Piscopals does, and had to read his prayers out of a book, instead of makin' 'em up once for all and then rec'-lectin' 'em word for word, as most people do. But he did pray, even if 'twas only book prayin', and he was always ready to go to the sick or troubled, and by his doctrines and his fruits we knew him to be a good man.

"And there's different kinds of Christians, after all. I didn't use to think so, and I know Elder Welcome never come to it. He thought there wasn't only one sort, and that was his. But I've seen things to make me think otherways. There's Jimmy Whitcher, of Francony—Fishin' Jimmy, 's they call him. I don't have a doubt he's been adopted, justified and sanctified in the most orthodox way. Nobody that knows him suspicions he hasn't. But I could wish, and so could a good many of us, that he was better grounded in the doctrines, and had set when young for a few years under Elder Welcome's solemn preachin'.

"Well, well, how I am spinnin' out this story! But you seem so interested, and everything comes back to me so, as we jog along through this section, that I can't stop talkin'. There ain't so very much more to tell, anyway. If you're lookin' for a sudden judgment on her, an awful vis'tation, like Lot's wife or Korah's proud troop, why you'll be disapp'inted. No, there wasn't anything like that, not even a death-bed repentance.

"Mehetabel wasn't ever very rugged in her health after that sickness of hers, and she had a good deal to try her afterwards. She worked pretty hard, and I suppose, after all, she missed her own home and folks some, and mebbe took to heart bein' so cut off and blamed by the church and c'mmunity. Anyway she begun to fail and run down, and didn't seem to have no great of strength. The children said she was homesick, that she kep' sayin' so.

"'Homesick for where?' asks they.

"'For the President's land,' she says, 'and the White House.'

"'I don't see,' says one, 'why you call it home, and what you want to go there so much for, anyway. You ain't got any folks there, have ye?'

"Oh yes,' she answers, 'lots and lots of folks.'

"'But not relations,' says another, 'not blood relations.'

"'Yes,' she says, smilin' to herself as if she knew more'n she could tell, 'that is just what they be, blood relations.'

"The boys and gals all felt sorry for her in those days, she looked so white and poor, and talked so much about wantin' to go home. 'Why don't you send word to the President about it?' says one of 'em, wantin' to humor her.

"'I do, time and time again,' she says. 'Oh, he knows!'

"'How does folks send word to him, anyway?' up and asks Ansel Peabody, seein' the weak p'ints of her story as well as a grown-up.

"'Oh, through his son allers, deary,' says Mehetabel. 'That's the only way there is, I guess."

"'S'pose folks don't know how to write,' says a little feller that hadn't learnt yet.

"'Why, they make their mark,' she says, 'and it does just as well.'

"One time she got the queerest idee in her head. Mis' Amos Bowles took her Sabbath-school class over to The Notch one day, and they come back full of the sights: Echo Lake and Bald Mountain and Profile Lake, and partic'lar The Profile itself. Now of course Mehetabel had seen that years before, but I don't believe she'd been there since her sickness, or she'd forgot or something. And when the boys and gals begun to tell about it and talked away of the Old Man o' the Mountain, and how he looked up there again' the sky and all that, why she seemed terrible int'rested. And after she'd heerd them tell how big and high and grand-like it was—most like a king, as some of 'em said—she took it into her head that 'twas a likeness, a sort of statue, I suppose, of her President. She asked 'em so many questions about it, and partic'lar about the kind of look the face wore, and they all agreed; and it's a fact, you know, that 'twas a hard featur'd, ha'sh-lookin', stony face.

"'But mebbe,' she says, 'you didn't look at it right; that makes such a dif-f'ence. I rec'lect,' she says, slow and hes-itatin', 's if she was tryin' to remember—' I rec'lect there was somethin', a long spell back, I used to look at the wrong way, and it scaret me, and—but I found out,' she says, brightenin' up, 'I'd jest been lookin' at it wrong side afore. Did you try every way?' she asks the children, 'and didn't the featur's sort o' change and get soft and forgivin' and lovin' any way you looked at 'em?' But they all said 'twasn't so, 'twas just a most hard featur'd, ha'sh-lookin' face from any p'int of view. She wouldn't take their word for it even then, but she kep' askin' other folks for days and days. She'd run out with her ap'on on her head and stop a team comin' back from The Notch, and she'd say, 'Did you see The Profile to-day? It's a real nice day,' she'd say, 'and the sun's out. Didn't the featur's kind o' lighten up 'fore you come away, and look softer and forgivin' and lovin'? But they never give her any satisfaction. So bimeby she made up her mind it couldn't be her President anyway, and it seemed to go out of her head.

"All that was in the summer. 'Twas a

hot, dry, drouthy season, and it seemed to pull her down a good deal. She was pleasant-spoken and comfortable-lookin' still—too much so for one that had ought to been weighed down with thoughts of her sinful state. But she often owned up to the children that she was dreadful lonesome and homesick, and pretty tired of the heat and the drouth. She talked to 'em about the President's country a good deal. From her account it must have been a real well-watered deestrict, for she told of springs and wells and fountains and brooks and rivers; one in partic'lar that run right down through the town, timbered all along the banks.

"Deary me! everything was just right in that place, accordin' to her. I'd like to find a section of country like it myself, and I'd settle there quick enough. Climate just temp'rate I should judge, for she said the sun wasn't ever too hot, the streams never dried up, 'twas allers good growin' weather, nobody felt the cold too much; and as for sickness, 'twan't known there.

" As I said, that fever of hers had took away all power of feelin' anything very strong, so she didn't exactly fret nor find fault, but she owned she couldn't hardly wait sometimes. I don't wonder, if she really believed in that place, that she did want to get off there. For she wasn't over-comfortable in Sugar Hill, sick and lonesome and poor and, more'n all, condemned by God and man.

" The boys and gals tried to cheer her up and divert her mind. 'Ma says you use to sing real nice, Aunt P'niel,' says Joey Barnes one day. 'She's heerd you in old times up to your pa's.'

" ' I disremember,' says she. ' I didn't think I ever sung any here in Sugar Hill. I sung a good deal at the President's.'

" ' Oh, sing us something, Aunt P'niel,'

they says, 'something you used to sing off there.'

"But she allers shook her head and says, 'No,' says she, 'you couldn't hardly expect me to sing the President's pieces here in Sugar Hill, where it's all so terrible different.'

"Old Tury was some comfort and company to her, I suppose; though she was a good deal of care, too, for she was gettin' old, and needed to be took charge of and watched. But she believed everything Mehetabel told her, and she'd heard it so frequent that she knew it by heart, and got to believin' she'd seen and heard it all herself, and knew the President and his son. And as Mehetabel grew weak and Tury grew old they'd sort of chirk one another up by goin' over this queer story. 'Much hot now,' Tury 'd say, 'much hot, Nyel'—that's what she called her—"sun burn Tury. Sun no hot Misser President's place?'

"'Oh no!' says Mehetabel, 'the sun never strikes folks there, not to hurt 'em any, though it's real light and shinin'.'

"'Water dry up now;' Tury 'd say; 'stream low, ground hard, grass all dry. Plenty stream there, Nyel?'

"'Yes, plenty, plenty, plenty,' Mehetabel 'd answer, 'and allers full, allers runnin' and cool and nice, and, oh, Tury, when I think of 'em I feel as thirsty as that deer we see tother day runnin' for Salmon Hole Brook!'

"'Injun there?' Tury asks one time. 'Misser Pres'dent let Injun come?'

"'Oh yes, yes, Tury,' Mehetabel says, 'all kinds o' folks that was ever made; he lets 'em all come, and glad to have 'em, too, and they all set up to one table together.'

"And Tury 'd grunt in that outlandish Injun way they do when they're pleased. 'Tury want flag, Nyel,' she says sometimes; 'Tury want wear Misser Pres'-

dent's mark, son's mark, so they know
Tury, let Tury in.'

"'Yes, I want that, too, dreadful bad,
Mehetabel 'd put in. 'We must get it
somehow or 'nother, Tury. Mebbe we'll
have it put on after we get there.'

"'Sign all white,' the old woman says.
'Tury see it on hill, shiny-white. Tury
get 'em put it on face, brown face; then
white mark show plain.'

"'Yes, it does look white up there on
Lafayette, don't it? But, Tury, seems to
me, as I rec'lect it, 'twas red there, in the
President's land; but mebbe I disremember.'

"'Flag white, Nyel; Tury never see
flag red,' she 'd say. And so they 'd go
on by the hour.

"We're drawin' nigh home now, and
there's the meetin'-house, off there; you
just see the steeple. But I'll drive slow,
for I guess we're goin' to have a nice
sunset to-night, and you seem int'rested

in such things. I don't notice 'em my-self much.

"Mehetabel failed pretty rapid that summer, and by September she took to her bed, and folks see she couldn't hold out much longer. Mr. Latham hadn't been up that year. He wanted to see the leaves turn, he wrote Mis' Peabody, and so he 'd wait till fall. About the last of September he come, and he felt dreadful bad when he found out how low Mehetabel Clark was. He spent most of his time there those days. He was alone with her and Tury a good deal, and no-body knows all the things that went on there among themselves. But I can't but hope, as a Christian minister, he tried to do his duty by that poor backslider, dyin' in her sins, and that deluded heathen in her blindness, as the hymn says.

"There was times, however, when other folks was there, too, and so I know a little about things. And they told me that there wasn't any change for the better in that poor soul, even at the very last. Elder Welcome acted like a Christian should, and let by-gones be by-gones, when he saw she was so nigh her end. He went to see her, and dealt with her faithful, for, he said, 'twasn't any time to shrink from a painful duty when she might be summoned any minute. So he held up the comin' judgment plain and strong, without slurrin' or smoothin' over. But he told me afterwards it done no good; she wouldn't pay any attention to what he said, nor ever lose her quiet, peaceable, smilin' look. That had all come back to her now, since she was so weak and low, and she didn't complain about bein' homesick or tired of things any more.

"The doctor thought she'd better be told that she couldn't live a great while longer; so she was. But her mind was wand'rin' a mite by that time, and she wouldn't believe what was told her. She used to smile in that old way of hers, as if she knew more'n anybody else about some things, and she'd say that she'd allers been told she shouldn't never die, and that she was goin' back to the President's land. She talked with the children when she was able, and they got the idee she thought she was goin' by water. And when they said they should think she'd be afraid, all alone, and her so unaccustomed to sailin', and it bein' cold weather now, she only whispered, for she hadn't much voice by that time, that she wa'n't a mite scaret, and she wasn't goin' alone.'

" There was a queer coincidence, as they say, about that time. She hadn't seen the White Cross, as you call it—that ledge and holler, as I say—since May or June, of course, and she'd set her mind on lookin' at it again. She'd keep askin' every day if the flag was up, and seemed to think she must hold on here till 'twas. Old Tury kep' tellin' her in her lingo that it couldn't be hung out till next spring, and Mr. Latham and the children and all tried to get her off the subject. It was a warm, soft fall, but about the first of October there come one of those sudden cold snaps we're liable to 'round here, and the thermometer fell fast.

"'Twas a bitter cold night, but in the mornin' the sun came out bright and warm again. Old Tury went up the road that afternoon, to Mis' Wells's, to get some milk they'd promised her, and when she come back she was in the craziest, excitedest state. She run into Mehetabel's room, and 'fore they could hush her or stop her she cries out, ' Flag out, Nyel, Misser Pres'dent's flag, son's flag, up on mountain !'

"And sure enough, it had snowed up there enough to pack that holler and lay again' the ledge, and the sun havin' thawed what was elsewhere 'round, there was the White Cross, as folks call it, pretty plain.

"Mehetabel took it very quiet. 'I knowed he'd put it up,' she whispered. Old Tury kep' goin' to the nearest p'int where she could catch a sight of Lafayette, so as to come back and tell Mehetabel. 'Flag there, Nyel,' she'd say, hobblin' in, 'no gone, flag there, shiny-white.'

"The last time she went 'twas nigh sundown, and Mr. Latham and some of the children went, and I was along, too; and there come just after the sun went down a kind of light we get here sometimes — I never see it anywhere else — a red, purply sort of color over everything; you know what I mean; I think we'll have it to-night, from the looks of things. And while we stood on the hill lookin' at Lafayette we see that purply color come creepin' over things. It touched the trees there on the Butter Hill road, and turned 'em yellerish-like first, and then pinky, and it went along there above the Profile Farm, and the side of Bald Mountain, and up and up Lafayette, makin' it all purply-red, and then on a sudden we see it had reached that ledge and holler.

" 'Twas queer, wasn't it, that it should have happened so, when Mehetabel had allers said she'd rec'lected the President's flag red instead of white? It seemed to fit into her story. And when old Tury run into her room and dropped down by the bed, and says, ' Flag red now, Nyel, flag red; Nyel say right, Misser Pres'-dent's flag red, son's flag red,' Meheta-bel's featur's took on a peaceabler look yet.

" I wasn't there at the very last. Mr. Latham was, and Tury, of course, but I never heard the partic'lars. A day or two beforehand one of the children told me he was there, and Aunt P'niel was most past speakin'. But he said Mr. Latham would read her little things sometimes, and again he'd say a word or two, and she'd rouse up and smile 's if she understood. And she'd got past hearin', too, I guess, for the boy said Mr. Latham made a kind of sign to her, and she smiled all over her face, and moved her lips, and old Tury she says, 'Flag, Nyel, Misser Pres'dent's flag, son's flag!' And so she was deluded to the very last."

The deacon's voice ceased; his story seemed ended. We were all very still, though thinking of many things. The wonderful purple light, which comes sometimes to those Franconia hills, was touching them now; and as we drove slowly along, facing old Lafayette, we saw the cross upon the mountain-side stained with crimson. The deacon saw it, too. He did not speak for some minutes. Then, suddenly, almost as if the words were forced from him in spite of himself, he said: "I've told you this about Mehetabel Clark as we here in the church and community have told it and looked at it—most of us—for all these years. It seemed the best, or, 't any rate, the least dang'rous way of puttin' it, and I've put it so to you to-day. But, mebbe, it ain't quite fair for me not to say, before I leave off, that sometimes, partic'lar since I'm growin' old, I find myself lookin' at things a mite different. There's times, and pretty frequent, too, when I get to thinkin' that mebbe, after all, there's another way than that old one of Elder Welcome's and ours, and that, somehow, she found it.

"I don't know how many times I've thought that, when I've been out in that little Sugar Hill buryin'-ground and seen Mehetabel's grave, just a little ways off from my Marietty's. It's so sort of still and hushed-up like there, as if 'twas waitin' for somethin', and—it makes me think of things. Mr. Latham took charge of buryin' her, you see, and he put up a stone. Some folks didn't think he done just right to put Scriptur' words over her, and I used to agree with 'em. But—I don't know. You must go and see it some day. There it is, cut on the marble cross as plain as day:

"'Thine eyes shall see the King in His beauty; they shall behold the land that is very far off.'"

www.ingramcontent.com/pod-product-compliance
Lightning Source LLC
Chambersburg PA
CBHW022146020726
47496CB00008B/2578

* 9 7 8 3 7 4 3 3 7 2 7 7 1 *